From the Stars in the Sky
to the Fish in the Sea

FROM THE STARS IN THE SKY TO THE FISH IN THE SEA
Copyright © 2017 by Kai Cheng Thom, Wai-Yant Li, and Kai Yun Ching

ARSENAL PULP PRESS
Suite 202 – 211 East Georgia St.
Vancouver, BC V6A 1Z6
Canada
arsenalpulp.com

The publisher gratefully acknowledges the support of the Canada Council for the Arts and the British Columbia Arts Council for its publishing program, and the Government of Canada (through the Canada Book Fund) and the Government of British Columbia (through the Book Publishing Tax Credit Program) for its publishing activities.

Printed and bound in Canada

Library and Archives Canada Cataloguing in Publication
Thom, Kai Cheng, author
        From the stars in the sky to the fish in the sea / Kai Cheng
Thom ; Wai-Yant Li, Kai Yun Ching, illustrators.

Issued in print and electronic formats.
ISBN 978-1-55152-709-3 (hardcover).—ISBN 978-1-55152-710-9 (HTML).
—ISBN 978-1-55152-711-6 (PDF)

        I. Li, Wai-Yant, illustrator II. Ching, Kai Yun, illustrator
III. Title.

PS8639.H559F76 2017   jC813'.6   C2017-903939-3
                                              C2017-903940-7

from the stars in the sky to the fish in the sea

written by
kai cheng thom

illustrated by
wai-yant li and kai yun ching

Arsenal Pulp Press
Vancouver

ONCE upon a time, in a little blue house on a hill on the edge of town, a baby was born. they were born when both the moon and the sun were in the sky, so the baby couldn't decide what to be.

boy or girl? bird or fish?
cat or rabbit? tree or star?
so the baby looked a little like
everything. they looked VERY
strange!

all the same, the baby's mother gave her child a bath and rocked them in her arms.

"your name," she said, "is Miu Lan." and she sang a song that her own mother had sung to her, long ago:

whatever you dream of,
i believe you can be,
from the stars in the sky
to the fish in the sea.
you can crawl like a crab
or with feathers fly high,
and i'll always be here,
i'll be near, standing by,
and you know that I'll love you
till the day that i die.

and even though they still couldn't decide, the
baby felt loved.

Miu Lan grew up to be a strange, magical child who was always changing.

they grew feathers and wings to fly
with bluebirds in the mornings,

scales and a tail to swim with
fish in the afternoons,

and fur and paws to play with
puppies in the evenings.

no matter how many things Miu Lan became, their mother always brought them back into the little blue house, gave them a bath, and tucked them into bed at the day's end. as the stars rose, she sang:

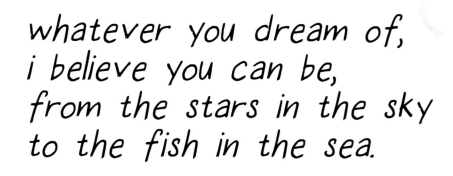

whatever you dream of,
i believe you can be,
from the stars in the sky
to the fish in the sea.

. . . and Miu Lan felt loved.

one day, it was time for the child to
go to school. they were so excited!
they grew a tail of peacock feathers
and a coat of tiger stripes.

"have fun," said Miu Lan's mother.
but when they got to the school . . !

the other students were either boys or girls: they had
no feathers, no scales, no leaves, no fur, no fins—not
even any sparkles! no one invited Miu Lan to play.

one little boy ran up to the child and asked, "what are you supposed to be?" Miu Lan didn't know how to answer.

when they came home, their mother asked them how they'd liked school.

"it's okay," said Miu Lan.
"did you make any friends?"
"not really," said Miu Lan.

that night, Miu Lan's mother tucked them into bed and
sang:

      you can crawl like a crab
      or with feathers fly high,
      and i'll always be here,
      i'll be near, standing by,
      and you know that i'll love you
      till the day that i die.

...and Miu Lan felt loved, but
also worried.

the next day, they wore a turtle shell and porcupine spines. no one pulled or poked Miu Lan, but the other children still pointed and whispered.

"did you make any friends today?" asked their mother.
"not really," said Miu Lan.

that night, Miu Lan's mother tucked them into bed and sang:

whatever you dream of,
i believe you can be,
from the stars in the sky
to the fish in the sea.

and Miu Lan felt loved.
but they also felt sad.

the next day, Miu Lan wore no feathers, no scales, no leaves, no fur, no fins, no shells, no spines—not even any sparkles. Miu Lan was invited to play baseball with the boys.

no one pointed, whispered, laughed, or stared. but when Miu Lan joined the little girls playing hopscotch—

"boys don't play hopscotch!" said a little girl.
"are you a boy or a girl, anyway?" asked a little boy.
"didn't you have a shell the other day?" asked a little
girl. "and feathers the day before?"

"what are YOU supposed to BE?"

said several children at once.

and galloped out of the playground on horse's hooves, swam through the stream with a fish's tail, and soared up the hill on an eagle's wings.

"how was school?"
asked Miu Lan's mother.

"i wore feathers and stripes so that the other kids would think i was beautiful, but they thought i was weird, and then i wore a shell and spines so that no one would pull or poke me, but they wouldn't talk to me, and then i tried to be just like everyone else, but i haven't made any friends. i can't decide what to be! why do i have to be just one thing?"

"it isn't always easy to be different from everyone else," said their mother.

"but you can only be who you are."

"what if the other children don't like who i am?" sniffled Miu Lan.

their mother smiled sadly.
"i don't know," she admitted, "but i do know this,"

whatever you dream of,
i believe you can be,
from the stars in the sky
to the fish in the sea.

. . . and Miu Lan felt loved.

that night, they slept a deep sleep.

the next day, Miu Lan wore fur, feathers, scales, leaves, and many sparkles that glittered like stars.

for a moment, none of the other children spoke. then a little girl said, "you can FLY? that's so cool!"

"i like your sparkles," said a little boy.
"i'm sorry i pulled your feathers," said the boy with red hair. "i was a little jealous of them."

Miu Lan asked, "does anyone want to play with me?"
they showed the other children how to gallop like
horses, climb like monkeys, and swim like fish.
it was fun to be many different things.

and the child of fur, feathers, scales, leaves, and sparkles who was neither boy nor girl, but many things and always changing, felt happy.

in the little blue house on the hill on the edge of town, Miu Lan's mother smiled and sang the song her mother had sung to her, once upon a time:

whatever you dream of,
i believe you can be,
from the stars in the sky to the fish in the sea.
you can crawl like a crab or with feathers fly high,
and i'll always be here, i'll be near, standing by,
and you know that i'll love you till the day that i die.
whatever you dream of,
i believe you can be,
for you are my child, courageous and free.

Dedication
To our parents

Acknowledgments

We are grateful to Brian, Oliver, Susan, and Cynara of Arsenal Pulp Press, whose belief and dedication have made this book possible. We also deeply indebted to the queer people of colour community of Montreal, whose love and brilliance have always been our inspiration, and to the Quilted Creatures collective, whose belief carried this project from its beginning.

Kai Cheng
My acknowledgements go out to my co-creators, Yun Ching and Wai-Yant, whose artistic vision gives shape to my words. I owe thanks as well to Kama, my beautiful soulmate, for her constant support—and to all my blood and chosen family in Vancouver, Montreal, and Toronto.

Yun Ching
My deepest gratitude goes out to Kai Cheng and Wai-Yant for a transformative and healing collaboration. This book was created with love for my dear sister, Jessica, and of course, Lisa, my oldest friend, and only because of the love and support of my dearest community.

Wai-Yant
To: my mom, dad, sister, and brother, for your support, patience, laughter, and belief in my journey; my chosen family who have stuck by me, thick and thin over many years; my community, whose voices have solidified my strength; my little nibling Leah Quyhn, for all your magical three-year-old guidance; and kai cheng thom and Yun Ching who have helped me grow superpowers with this collaboration and love. Thank you.